THE DISGUSTING ADVENTURES OF

FLEABAG MONKEYFACE

THE TEMPLE OF BABOON

WALKER
BOOKS

KNIFE &
PACKER

The authors would like to dedicate this book
to the inventor of the holiday, without whom
there would be no time off school!

First published 2011 by Walker Books Ltd
87 Vauxhall Walk, London SE11 5HJ

2 4 6 8 10 9 7 5 3

© 2011 Duncan McCoshan and Jem Packer

The right of Duncan McCoshan and Jem Packer to be identified
as author/illustrator of this work has been asserted by them
in accordance with the Copyright, Designs and Patents Act 1988

This book has been typeset in Shinn Light

Printed and bound in Great Britain by Clays Ltd, St Ives plc

British Library Cataloguing in Publication Data:
a catalogue record for this book is available
from the British Library

ISBN 978-1-4063-2434-1

www.walker.co.uk
www.knifeandpacker.com

But before we get to the horrible smelly stuff, let's meet our heroes, **Gerald**, **Gene** and **Fleabag Monkeyface**. Here's a few things you need to know about them:

Gerald
Likes: The sound of a toilet flushing
Dislikes: Clean towels
Favourite word: "Cool"
You should know:
Gerald has the stupid habit of liking Gene's ideas

Gene
Likes: Making lists, especially of gross things
Dislikes: Bunny rabbits
Favourite word: "Unreal"
You should know:
Gene has the ideas

Fleabag Monkeyface
Likes: Eating nits
Dislikes: Baths, showers and soap
Favourite word: "Ug-brilliant"
You should know:
He's got Gross-Out Power

Without Gerald, Gene and Fleabag, the world would be a much cleaner, shinier place. But let's start at the beginning...

"**W**elcome to the five-star Hotel Dorado," said the hotel manager as he escorted Gerald, Gene and Fleabag Monkeyface to their luxurious room. (Gerald's mum had won a beach holiday in the exotic South American country of Bolividor.)

"Unreal!" said Gene, bouncing on the huge bed.

"Cool!" said Gerald, admiring the sea view.

"Ug-clean, ug-air-conditioned, ug-luxurious... I ug-hate it!" said Fleabag, opening his suitcase. "Thank ug-goodness I packed my **pet worm, Iggy** – he'll remind me of home!"

Gerald, Gene and Fleabag's love of gross out was always getting them into trouble, and this wasn't the first time they'd taken something gross on holiday with them...

UNREAL!

Gerald had once packed a set of his granny's false teeth for a ski trip...

COOL!

Gene had once filled a rucksack with smelly socks for a city break...

UG-BRILLIANT!

And **Fleabag Monkeyface** had once taken an entire nit circus on a hill-walking holiday.

"Did you know that explorers discovered a **lost kingdom** here a couple of hundred years ago?" said Gerald, reading a local guidebook by the pool a couple of days later. "'This mythical land is said to be home to tribes of wild monkeys, giant squid and the legendary Temple of Baboon.'"

"Wow! We should go," said Gene.

"We can't," said Gerald. "All maps were lost centuries ago. One explorer – **Montana Smith** – set off to rediscover the kingdom recently, but he hasn't been seen since. The place does sound amazing, though. Listen to this..."

The Legend of the Golden

Centuries ago, terrifying Zombie Monkeys terrorized the Lost Kingdom of Smell Dorado and the monkeys who lived there. They planned to conquer the whole world...

The zombies were finally defeated when one brave and defiant monkey took the Elixir of Yuck – a potion said to give huge strength and power to the drinker. This monkey became the great primate warrior Chimpzilla!

Chimpzilla flushed the Zombie Monkeys down the Temple's sacred Golden Toilet and then cast a spell that banished them to live for ever beneath the earth's surface.

Toilet of Smell Dorado

But Chimpzilla's spell had a fatal flaw...

And every 100 years, on the day of the full solar eclipse, the spell is broken!

Then the indestructible Golden Toilet becomes a gateway into the world above, and no matter where it is, the Zombie Monkeys emerge ... ready to cause mayhem once again!

Fortunately, Chimpzilla's spell has been passed down from tribe leader to tribe leader. At each eclipse, this leader, known as the Baboon King, recasts the spell...

This spell gives the Baboon King – or whoever speaks it – power over the Zombie Monkeys. And for centuries, at the king's command, the Zombie Monkeys have gone back into the Toilet and been flushed away once more ... until the next eclipse!

"That place sounds amazing," said Gene. "Fleabag would love it. **A warrior monkey!**"

"Talking of Fleabag, what *is* he doing?" asked Gerald.

Fleabag was hard at work at the far end of the beach, and Gerald and Gene went to investigate what he was up to.

(Now if you have read a Fleabag Monkeyface book before, you will know that Fleabag lives in the **Gross-Out Den**, which is really an old disused toilet at the end of Gerald's garden.)

Gerald and Gene, who were a bit bored of all the luxury and cleanliness, were glad to be back in *their* kind of surroundings.

Fleabag, meanwhile, had turned his attention to his pet worm, Iggy. "I'm ug-training him to ug-grab things from high shelves!" he said, holding up his arm – Iggy was wrapped affectionately around his hairy wrist.

Just then, there was a knock on the wall of the Den.

"Buffet o'clock, guys!" called Gerald's dad.

"And look what I found," added Gerald's mum, holding up a leaflet.

Gerald's parents were always trying to get the boys to go on "exciting" excursions. These usually involved something boring like a sunset cruise or a visit to a local craft fair. But when the friends saw this leaflet they were very excited!

BARON VON DIRTHOFFEN'S TRAVELLING MUSEUM OF GROSS!

The world's greatest living grossaeologist
will be displaying artefacts from his

TRAVELLING MUSEUM OF GROSS.

And don't miss the world premier!

BE THE FIRST TO SEE

the museum's newest and most prized artefact:
The recently (and locally) discovered ...

GOLDEN TOILET OF SMELL DORADO!

"The Golden Toilet of Smell Dorado!" gasped Gene. "So it *does* exist!"

"I've got you tickets for tomorrow," said Gerald's mum.

"Cool!" said Gerald. "This is so much better than that Rainforest Fauna and Flora Rafting Trip you had wanted us to go on!"

"But I thought Smell Dorado didn't exist and the **Golden Toilet** was just a legend," mused Gene. "How did the baron get there – and how did he escape alive...?"

2 Meanwhile, on the other side of town, a convoy of lorries was pulling up in an empty parking lot. **The Travelling Museum of Gros$** had arrived...

"How I hate zis place," said a tall, thin, nasty looking man. He turned to his nephew, a small rotund boy called Melvin. "You get to work *und* I vill relax in the office. Call me when it's time to unload the Toilet!"

BARON VON DIRTHOFFEN'S TRAVELLING MUSEUM OF GROSS!

Although the baron did not intend to lift a finger to help set up, there was one box that he alone was going to put in place.

"I'm not letting zis out of my sight for a minute," he said later as he placed an armour-plated box on a plinth. "*Mein* precious toilet."

And, with shaking hands, he opened the box to reveal the magnificent artefact.

"I can't believe we have it, Uncle," breathed Melvin.

"*Ve? Ve* don't have anything," snapped the baron. "*I* have the **Golden Toilet**, *und* soon I vill have EVERYTHING I HAVE EVER DREAMED OF!!! Now, it's **Sausage Time!**"

Back in the office, Melvin and the baron sat down to a late supper.

"Good thing I always travel *mit mein* own bratwurst," said the baron, tucking into a large sausage. "Ze local food is disgusting."

"The mobile bratwurst fridge was a brainwave," said Melvin. "So much better than eating the native stuff."

"I am full of good ideas," gloated the baron. "And thanks to the **Golden Toilet**, I vill soon be able to realize them all. No more travelling for me! No more setting up ze museum in a different town every few days. **Oh no! SOON I VILL BE KNOWN AS SO MUCH MORE THAN JUST *EIN* TRAVELLING SHOWMAN!!!**"

"Tell me more, Uncle," begged Melvin.

"Not now. *Ich bin* tired," said Von Dirthoffen, tucking into yet another sausage. "But make no mistake, it vill be HUGE!"

"And what about our 'visitor'?" said Melvin. "Should I take him something to eat? He has been in that box for four days..."

The baron's eyes bulged and he barked angrily: "If you must! Here, take him this crust of bread *und* the end of this sausage. Oh, *und* remind him that **this isn't a hotel!**"

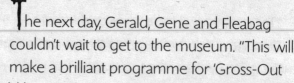

3

The next day, Gerald, Gene and Fleabag couldn't wait to get to the museum. "This will make a brilliant programme for 'Gross-Out TV'!" Gerald beamed as he packed up their film gear.

("Gross-Out TV" was Gerald, Gene and Fleabag's very own TV show – but their adventures always seemed to get in the way of them making programmes.)

"Hurry ug-up, you ug-guys!" Fleabag said as he finished making himself a mouldy coconut sandwich for the trip. "The minibus leaves in five ug-minutes!"

The minibus bumped along some dirt roads. Before long it pulled up at the museum. There to meet the party was a small, geeky looking boy.

WELCOME AND GREETINGS! I AM MELVIN VON DIRTHOFFEN, NEPHEW OF THE WORLD'S GREATEST GROSSAEOLOGIST! YOU LUCKY PEOPLE ARE THE FIRST TO SEE THE MUSEUM'S LATEST AND GREATEST ACQUISITION.

PEOPLE SAID IT DIDN'T EXIST – BUT WE SEARCHED FOR YEARS AND FINALLY REDISCOVERED THE TREACHEROUS LOST KINGDOM OF SMELL DORADO. WE CROSSED PERILOUS RAVINES AND BATTLED GREAT BEASTS TO BRING YOU OUR MOST FANTASTIC EXHIBIT EVER...

BUT WE'LL SAVE THAT FOR THE GRAND FINALE. FIRST OF ALL FOLLOW ME – AND PREPARE TO BE ASTOUNDED BY THE FINEST COLLECTION OF GROSS ANTIQUITIES EVER SEEN...

Gerald, Gene and Fleabag couldn't believe their eyes: room after room of **ancient gross-out marvels** ... and they were getting it all on film!

23

"Now, ladies and gentlemen," said Melvin, as the crowd gathered together outside a locked door. "It is time for the grand finale..."

But just then something terrible happened – Iggy decided to go "walkabout"...

"What is that *thing*?!" cried Melvin as the worm crawled across the floor. "Stop it at once!"

"Iggy! Ug-come back!" Fleabag shouted, desperately chasing after his beloved pet.

Gerald and Gene tried to help by lunging for the rogue worm, but they slipped and slammed into the base of a huge pole.

"**The Grossempole!**" cried Melvin as a massive totem pole started to shudder and wobble. "That priceless antique is over 300 years old!"

"It's going to come down!" cried Gene. "Time for some **Gross-Out Power, Fleabag!**"

Fleabag immediately sprang into action.

"Ug-supersonic sneeze!" he cried, and with an antique-shuddering ATCHOO!, he aimed a sneeze at the top of the totem pole.

The pole stopped toppling. The crowd breathed a sigh of relief ... until a second later, when it started wobbling again!

"Try something stronger!" shouted Gerald.

"Bionic earwax pellets!" Fleabag shrieked.

The pellets hit their target, and the **Grossempole** finally settled back into place.

The priceless exhibits were safe!

"Well done, Fleabag! You saved the museum!" Gerald cheered.

"And I saved ug-Iggy," said Fleabag, smiling at his beloved grub.

But before the crowd could celebrate, a door behind them clanked open.

"What is all *das* commotion?!" said a tall man, appearing in the doorway.

Gerald, Gene and Fleabag immediately recognized him from the leaflet. It was **Baron Von Dirthoffen** himself!

"You are about to vitness the greatest ever archaeological find *und* you are messing around!" the baron groaned.

"We can explain—" Gene began.

"Quiet *und* silence," Von Dirthoffen cried. "*Und* I vant zat film gear. No filming in zis room! Now come in and see *mein* precious Toilet!"

4

The baron led the way into a small room. The crowd gasped, and Gerald, Gene and Fleabag forgot about their missing film gear.

In a glass cabinet on a velvet plinth sat a small but intricately carved golden toilet.

"Don't get too close," warned the baron. "It is protected by a system of security lasers."

"Wow!" breathed Gerald.

"But how did you find it?" Gene asked. "No one has been to **Smell Dorado** for centuries – except Montana Smith, and he never returned."

"Montana Smith, paaah!" said the baron. "Zat man is *ein* fake *und ein* charlatan!"

"It was uncle and I who made the perilous journey into that cursed land," added Melvin. "We battled—"

"Enough!" shrieked Von Dirthoffen. "Exit via *das* gift shop. We are expecting more tourists." And with that he and Melvin shooed the crowd from the room.

"Well, that was amazing!" said Gene, paying for a postcard. "Smell Dorado must be some place! I wonder if the baron knows about the legend of the Zombie Monkeys—"

"Hang on," interrupted Gerald, "where's Fleabag?"

"He must still be in the museum," said Gene.

The pair quickly snuck back inside. They soon located Fleabag – he was sitting on the **Golden Toilet**! "When you've got to go, you've got to ug-go!" he explained sheepishly.

Just then an alarm sounded and a familiar voice boomed across the room: "You set off *das* alarm!" It was the baron. "Now, get off *mein* toilet, this is *ein* OUTRAGE! How dare you!"

5 "I'm ug-sorry, Mr Baron, but I've really got to ug-go," pleaded Fleabag.

There was a loud gurgling noise that startled even the world's leading grossaeologist.

"Maybe there's a staff toilet?" implored Gene.

"He could destroy the museum!" added Gerald.

"Very vell," said the baron reluctantly. "This way."

But suddenly Melvin burst into the room. "Uncle, it's an emergency!" he hollered. "The cash register in the gift shop has broken down!"

"Must I do *everything* around here?" the baron sighed. "*Me*, the vorld's most famous grossaeologist!" He turned to Fleabag. "The toilet is through zis door, but be quick, *und* no schnooping."

Gerald, Gene and Fleabag went through the door
and found themselves in a corridor full of crates.
The staff toilet was at the end of the hall, and Fleabag
rushed towards it. He slammed the door behind him.

"Block your ears," said Gene. "This could be noisy!"

But instead of hearing Fleabag on the toilet, Gerald
and Gene heard a different kind of noise.

"What *is* that?" asked Gerald. "It sounds like a
voice."

"It can't be Fleabag, surely!" said Gene.

There was a loud **FLUSH!**

"That's ug-better," said Fleabag, emerging from the toilet with a broad smile on his hairy face. "But I think I'll give the ug-double spicy burritos a miss tonight—"

Fleabag was interrupted by the same noise Gerald and Gene had heard – but this time it was louder!

"The ug-museum's haunted!" cried Fleabag. "We must ug-escape!"

"Not so fast," said Gene. "Someone's in here."

"Behind those crates," said Gerald. "Next to the statue of the **Carthaginian Latrine Demon**."

The three friends quickly pushed the statue back to reveal a metal cage. In it, a man was hunched in a corner.

"**Montana Smith. International archaeological man-of-action,**" he said. "I'm being kept prisoner by the baron and his nasty nephew. You have to help me! Now, listen very carefully. We don't have much time..."

"I have known the baron since childhood. We shared a love of digging – but even then he always had to outdo me...

"As we grew older, the rivalry grew as well. And while I was interested in uncovering and recording the past, the baron was motivated only by greed. Whenever I made a **gross-out discovery** he was right behind me, ready to steal it from me...

"Finally, he opened his own Travelling Museum to display all his stolen artefacts...

"And when I finally found the path to the **Lost Kingdom of Smell Dorado**, the baron and his nephew were right behind me...

"Apart from my necklace – given to me by a native – I took nothing from that sacred land. But the baron was there to loot!

"After forcing me to lead him to the Temple of Baboon, he stole the **Golden Toilet** and extracted an ancient spell from the Baboon King by force.

"Now the baron is terrified I will return the Toilet, so he is keeping me locked up."

"I don't know exactly what he is planning," concluded Montana. "But we must get the Toilet back to the Baboon King before the solar eclipse—"

"Or Zombie Monkeys will emerge and take over the earth?" interrupted Gene.

"So you know the legend. I suspect the baron is hoping to use them somehow. But he must be stopped! The Toilet must be returned to the king! The baron must not be allowed to say the spell!!!"

"Hey, are you finished in zere?" cried Baron Von Dirthoffen. He was back from fixing the cash register!

"We need to go," said Gerald urgently.

"We can't leave Montana!" said Gene.

"There's no time," said the archaeologist. "You have to go *now*. If the baron catches you, it's all over. *You* must return the **Golden Toilet** to Smell Dorado! Here, this map will help you."

"We'll come back and free you," said Gene.

"No. It's too dangerous. If the baron and his nephew notice I'm gone, they'll come after me. Our only hope is to get the Toilet back to the Temple of Baboon without them suspecting anything. Now, hurry, you don't have much time... **The next solar eclipse is in TWO DAYS!**"

Gerald, Gene and Fleabag were soon back at the Tropical Gross-Out Den examining the map Montana had given them...

FOLLOW THIS ROUTE

FLESH-EATING CRABS

FISH-HEAD FALLS

VALLEY OF PUTRID PLANTS

CONCEALED ENTRANCE

TOXIC GORGE OF DEADMAN'S DROOL

HOTEL DORADO

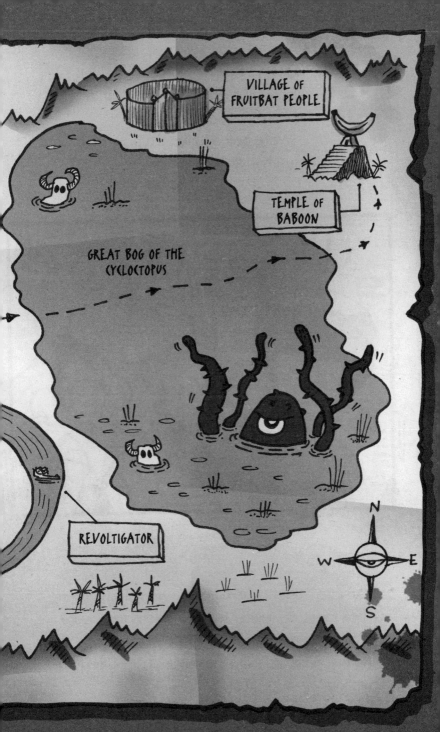

6 "So we need to ug-steal a golden toilet and ug-enter a mythical land?" said Fleabag. "Sounds like ug-fun!"

"We're going to need a plan," said Gene. "And I've just had an idea..."

"An idea? Cool!" said Gerald – who always liked Gene's ideas, no matter how ridiculous they were.

"I'll need a pile of your earwax, Fleabag," said Gene. "And that postcard from the museum. It's time to get sculpting!"

Despite interruptions from Gerald's parents (who kept suggesting more boring excursions, including trips to a tapestry-weaving factory and an avocado farm), Gerald, Gene and Fleabag worked hard, and by the end of the next day they were ready.

"Behold the **Earwax Toilet of Smell Dorado**!" Gene beamed. "Now all we have to do is swap it for the original and then return that to the lost kingdom!"

"So we're going back to the ug-museum?" said Fleabag. "I'll make an ug-packed lunch!"

"There's no time for that," said Gene. "The museum closes in an hour. We need to get there as soon as we can. You saw the locks on the doors – there will be no way in after it shuts."

"The replacement toilet is good," said Gerald, "but we can't just walk in and swap it in broad daylight. The baron will recognize us from yesterday."

"We're going to go as tacky tourists," said Gene. "And I know just where we can get the clothes..."

7 First they went to Gerald's dad, who was sitting by the pool, to borrow one of his ridiculously bright holiday shirts.

Then they went to Gerald's mum, who was sipping a pineapple-and-cumquat cocktail on the terrace of the hotel bar, to borrow some of her unnecessarily big sunglasses.

WE DON'T WANT ANY UNNECESSARILY BIG SUNGLASSES...

BUT IF WE COULD JUST HAVE SOME OF YOURS, MUM.

And finally they went to Fernando the flamboyant cocktail waiter to borrow some garish Bermuda shorts.

Gerald, Gene and Fleabag were now dressed from head to toe in loud holiday-wear.

"Loving the look!" Gene beamed. "Melvin and the baron will never recognize us now."

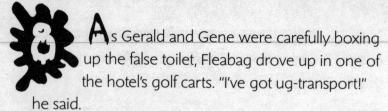

As Gerald and Gene were carefully boxing up the false toilet, Fleabag drove up in one of the hotel's golf carts. "I've got ug-transport!" he said.

"Cool!" said Gerald, and they set off for the museum, leaving Gerald's parents to enjoy the cabaret by the pool.

"Now comes the tricky part," said Gene as they pulled up outside the museum. "We act like tacky tourists and swap the toilets as soon as possible."

Luckily, their absurd disguises worked perfectly, and they snuck through the exhibition undetected.

"We just need to wait for everyone to leave so we can make the change," said Gene, as Baron Von Dirthoffen repeated his talk about the **Golden Toilet**.

Unfortunately, the baron had been rattled by the previous morning's incident and was determined that no more visitors would go poking about.

"No dawdling!" he said, shepherding the visitors into the gift shop. "Zat applies to you too, ze threesome in *das* loud shirts!"

"We need a diversion," whispered Gerald.

"I know just the thing!" said Gene. "What is he most concerned about?"

"The gift shop and its takings," said Gerald. "Perfect!"

Gene knew the baron wouldn't be able to resist a wealthy tourist spending loads of money in his shop.

Fleabag got to work immediately.

I AM AN UG-RICH BUSINESS MAN. I WANT TO BUY UG-GIFTS FOR ALL MY FAMILY AND I HAVE A **VERY** UG-LARGE FAMILY...

"Seventeen 'I've been to Baron Von Dirthoffen's Travelling Museum' T-Shirts, fourteen ug-replica Phoenician nose-pickers, twelve Inca potty deity statuettes, thirty-five Smell Dorado snow shakers," he ordered.

And while the baron and his nephew were busy getting his order from the storeroom, Fleabag quickly turned off the security system...

Meanwhile, Gerald and Gene had crept back into the museum. And as soon as the security system around the Toilet was down, Gerald prised open the cabinet and grabbed the **Golden Toilet of Smell Dorado**.

"Quick!" urged Gene. "Make the switch!"

Gerald handed him the real toilet and then carefully put the fake one in its place.

"We did it!" Gene cried.

But now they had to retrieve Fleabag...

"That *ist* everything," said the baron, who was out of breath from piling up all the merchandise.

"Have it delivered to the Hotel Dorado," said Gene.

"Yes – I have an ug-urgent business meeting to attend," Fleabag added with a flourish.

And with that they were off – the **Golden Toilet** safely stowed away in Gene's rucksack.

"Well, that's the easy part done," said Gene ominously once they were back in the **Tropical Gross-Out Den**. "Now it gets *really* hard. We've got to get this back to the Temple of Baboon."

"What do you mean, ug-hard?" said Fleabag, examining Montana's map. "Stinking swamps, man-ug-eating plants, giant ug-creepy crawlies – now that sounds like MY kind of ug-holiday resort!"

"Yes, but how do we get there?" said Gene.

"Hang on," said Gerald. "Part of that map looks familiar. Where's that leaflet my parents gave us – the one for the rafting trip? You remember: rainforest, fauna, flora..."

"There's so ug-many," said Fleabag, riffling through the stack of leaflets he'd stashed behind the toilet. "You mean this ug-one?"

Gerald held up the leaflet.

Rainforest Fauna & Flora Rafting Trip

Get up close and personal with some of Bolividor's finest fauna and flora!

"The rafting route goes right past the hidden entrance to Smell Dorado!" said Gerald.

"Pack your swimming costumes – we're going rafting!" added Gene.

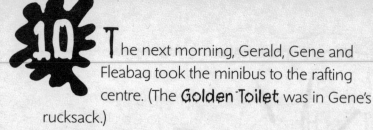

10

The next morning, Gerald, Gene and Fleabag took the minibus to the rafting centre. (The **Golden Toilet** was in Gene's rucksack.)

Unfortunately, though, the boys weren't the only ones on the trip...

OH NO!
IT'S THE
SMUGLEYS!

There, in full tropical outfits, were Randy and Mandy Smugley, the twins who lived next door to Gerald back home. The Smugleys were the complete opposite of Gerald, Gene and Fleabag and loved all things soft and fluffy.

"What are *you* doing here?" asked a horrified Gene.

"We're in Bolividor on a field trip. We're collecting tropical flowers for our pressed flower collection," said Mandy.

"Bolividor has some of the finest orchids in the world," added Randy.

And before Gerald, Gene and Fleabag could find another boat, their raft was off, zooming down the river.

"Now, listen up!" said the guide. "My name is Ernesto and I am in charge, so if you would like to stop for any reason please let me know!"

The Smugleys wanted to stop every five minutes to collect flowers for their collection.

"This is taking too long," said Gene.

"The entrance to Smell Dorado should be around the next bend," said Gerald, looking at the map.

And squinting up at the mountainside, they could just make out the outline of an entrance.

"There it is," said Gerald. "Ernesto, we need to get off here."

"What a lovely spot!" gushed Mandy.

"How are we going to get ug-rid of *them*?" hissed Fleabag.

"Randy, Mandy," said Gene, thinking quickly. "I think there are some ... er ... Lesser Spotted ... er ... Fairy Plum Orchids over there."

"*Fairy Plum* Orchids?" gasped Randy. "Only the rarest orchid in the world!"

11

With the Smugleys distracted, Gerald, Gene and Fleabag were able to head for the entrance to Smell Dorado. They climbed up a hill and came to a stop in front of the unmistakable outline of a door.

"Now ... somewhere around here there should be a small sculpture of a monkey's head..." said Gene. "It operates the gates."

"Ug-over here!" Fleabag pointed.

Just then they heard voices behind them.

"Yoo-hoo! "

"Where are you?"

It was the Smugleys!

"The gates won't open!" cried Gene, tugging desperately on the monkey-head lever.

"Let me have an ug-go," said Fleabag. "I'm ug-good with all matters monkey." He gently tickled the sculpture's nose and this time something *did* happen...

The ground beneath them began to shake and shudder, and suddenly the vast cliff-face parted...

"The gateway to the Lost Kingdom of Smell Dorado!" gasped Gerald.

SCREECH!

SCRAPE!

61

They hurried through the vast rock gates, which slammed shut behind them. They had escaped the Smugleys!

Below them lay Smell Dorado...

"Wow! This place is like nothing on earth!" said Gerald.

"Ug-home from home," said Fleabag.

"Now to the Temple," said Gene, looking at the map. "First we've got to get down into the valley."

"So where're the ug-stairs?" said Fleabag. "Or is there an ug-lift?"

"I don't think you'll find either of them here, Fleabag," said Gerald, looking over the edge of the cliff. "How *are* we going to get down?"

For once, Gene was out of ideas. Luckily, Fleabag piped up: "I've been working on a new ug-Gross-Out Power... **Nose-Hair Power!**"

"Nose-Hair Power?" asked Gerald. "How does *that* work?"

"It's a bit ug-like abseiling," said Fleabag. "Ug-hold on to my nose hair and I'll ug-lower you down."

Although it sounded like the grossest mode of transport ever, Gerald and Gene didn't have a choice. Fleabag took a deep breath and, with a loud snort, a rope of knotted nose hair appeared from his nostrils.

"Now ug-hold on," he said.

Gerald and Gene clung on and Fleabag lowered them into the valley.

"Easy does it," said Gene. He was terrified the **Golden Toilet** would get damaged.

"We're there!" said Gerald as they reached the jungle floor.

It was now Fleabag's turn, and, wrapping the nose hair around a large rock, he abseiled down.

"Well done, Fleabag," said Gene. **"Great nose power!"**

"It was a bit ug-sore, but I knew I could do it," said Fleabag proudly.

"So where do we go now?" Gerald asked Gene, who was studying the map.

"There should be a path just beyond that boulder," said Gene. "We need to stay close together. This is going to be dangerous..."

12 Back at the museum, the baron was
doing his two favourite things: counting the
museum's takings and eating a sausage.

"I have the day's total, Uncle," said Melvin,
looking up from his calculator. "Uncle," he repeated.
"I have the museum's takings!"

"Ah, yes, I vas miles away," said the baron, chuckling
slyly. "I was thinking about my plan. The time grows
closer *und* closer."

"Oh, the *plan*," said Melvin. "Are you going to tell
me about that now?"

"Very well," said the baron. "But hold on to the cash register receipt, this is going to blow your shoes *auf*!" The baron's eyes lit up as he went on: "In less than 24 hours, it will be the solar eclipse and Zombie Monkeys will emerge from the **Golden Toilet**, right here in the museum."

"So the legend of the Zombie Monkeys is true!" said Melvin.

OH YES! AND UNDER **MY** COMMAND ZEY WILL NOT RETURN TO THE UNDERWORLD. OH NO! I VILL ORDER THEM TO RANSACK EVERY MUSEUM IN THE WORLD.

THEY WILL DESTROY ALL THOSE BORING PICTURES AND SCULPTURES AND THEN I WILL FILL ALL THE MUSEUMS WITH MY ARTEFACTS. SOON WE WILL HAVE THE GROSSENHEIM IN NEW YORK, THE NATIONAL GROTTERY IN LONDON, THE LOUVATORY IN PARIS, AND MANY MORE!

EVERY MUSEUM WILL BECOME A VON DIRTHOFFEN MUSEUM OF GROSS! MONTANA SMITH WILL BOW BEFORE ME *UND* I VILL BE RICH *UND* FAMOUS **WORLDVIDE!!!!**

13 Unaware of the baron's monstrous plan, Gerald, Gene and Fleabag were trying to get to the **Temple of Baboon**. New perils lurked around every corner. Strange animals appeared from bushes, huge lizard-like birds buzzed in trees overhead and vast creepy crawlies covered every leaf.

And there was worse to come...

They were almost eaten alive in the **Valley of Putrid Plants**...

They were almost melted by deadly phlegm as they crossed the **Toxic Gorge of Deadman's Drool**...

They were exhausted and battered, but Gerald, Gene and Fleabag had made it through the first set of obstacles that Smell Dorado had to offer. Their journey was far from over, though, and once again they set off in the direction of the Temple...

"**U**ncle, come quickly!" wheedled Melvin. "The **Golden Toilet** ... it's ... it's melting!"

"Melting? *Das ist* not possible," cried the baron. "It is made of solid gold!"

But, sure enough, the Toilet was slowly softening and dissolving...

Von Dirthoffen yanked open the cabinet door to have a closer look. "This *ist ein* impostor!" he shrieked. "Someone has taken *mein* precious Toilet *und* replaced it with one made from—"

"Earwax!" said Melvin, scrunching up his nose in disgust. "But who?"

"Montana Smith must be behind this!" boomed the Baron. "I vill have a little chat with him while you look through the security-camera footage. Ve don't have much time – ze eclipse *ist* today!"

The baron headed straight to Montana's cage.
"*Mein* toilet *ist* gone!" he barked. "I know you must be behind zis! You have arranged for someone to steal it and return it to the Baboon King – but who?"

"I'm not saying anything," said the brave explorer, who was delighted to hear that Gerald, Gene and Fleabag had succeeded in the first part of the plan.

Just then Melvin called to his uncle. "Come quick! You must see this!"

"I vill deal *mit* you later," the baron said to Montana. He followed Melvin to the office.

"It was the two tourists from yesterday afternoon!" Melvin said, showing his uncle the footage from the CCTV camera. "They stole the Toilet while the third one was distracting us. And look – they bear a remarkable resemblance to the threesome who used the staff toilet the previous day."

"Montana must have put them up to zis," said Von Dirthoffen. "Vell, we vill simply hunt them down before zey get to the Temple. **PREPARE ZE GROSSEMPOLE – we are going back to Smell Dorado!**"

15 "I have made a few repairs since our last trip and boosted its power," said Melvin proudly, as they approached the tall, wooden structure.

"Excellent, excellent," said Von Dirthoffen. "Prepare the vehicle for immediate departure. And don't forget to fill the fridge!"

Melvin pressed a hidden switch on the side of the tall sculpture and an amazing transformation began to occur...

The totem-pole face retracted to reveal a cockpit and two steering wheels.

Helicopter blades began to whirr while sophisticated tracking equipment, hidden in the headdress, mapped out the route to Smell Dorado.

Destructo-arms, for bashing forests and enemies, emerged.

A super-powerful grabbing hand appeared.

A solar-powered fridge for fresh and tasty bratwurst powered up.

A hovercraft engine ignited. It was able to propel the vehicle through any terrain.

Once inside the cockpit of the Grossempole, the baron sighed. "I thought we would never return to zat awful place. **I hate Smell Dorado!**"

"And what will we do when we get there?" asked Melvin.

"First we get our **Golden Toilet** back," said Von Dirthoffen. "Then as soon as the eclipse happens, I will command ze Zombie Monkeys as planned. Now, pass me a sausage. I'm super-peckish, *ja*!"

16

Meanwhile, in Smell Dorado, the terrain had changed from dense rainforest to marshy swamp.

"We have to cross the **Great Bog of the Cycloctopus**," said Gene

"I don't like the sound of a 'Cycloctopus'," Gerald sighed. He'd already had enough of Smell Dorado's "exotic" wildlife.

"With my ug-worm whip there is nothing to ug-fear!" said Fleabag bravely. "Iggy and I will ug-turn that Cycloctopus into sushi..."

The **Great Bog of the Cycloctopus** was very squelchy. It was hard to walk through. Plus, the threesome had the uncomfortable feeling that they were being watched...

"There – up ahead – I can see a path!" said Gerald.
Sure enough, the end of the bog was in sight.
But before they could reach dry ground, the
Cycloctopus struck!

"Help!" cried Gene as large tentacles gripped his legs and pulled him backwards.

"It won't let go!" said Gerald as he kicked the huge, wobbly beast.

"Oh no – it's got Iggy!" said Fleabag as his worm was snatched from his grasp.

"It seems to be taking us somewhere," gasped Gene. "But where?"

17

On the other side of Smell Dorado, the great gates were once again creaking open.

"Back again. *Bleurgh!*" said Baron Von Dirthoffen, holding his nose. "Not only is it *über* dangerous, but zat smell!"

"Yes, but by nightfall, the Zombie Monkeys will be wrecking every museum in the world!" said Melvin.

"True, true, nephew," said the baron. "So where are the three thieves *und* where is *mein* toilet?!"

"The atmospherics aren't showing anything," Melvin complained as he fiddled with switches and adjusted knobs on the Grossempole's advanced tracking equipment.

"I feared this vould not be easy," said the baron. "Ve will simply have to get to the Temple of Baboon *und* wait for them zere. Onwards!"

18 The Cycloctopus had Gerald, Gene and Fleabag firmly in its grasp and was dragging them back into the bog.

"What does it want with us?!" cried Gerald.

"Are we going to be its ug-dinner?!" wailed Fleabag.

"Maybe it's taking us back to its lair!" said Gene.

But instead the Cycloctopus dumped them at the gates of a village...

"We're saved! We're ug-saved!" shouted Fleabag joyously. (He'd even got Iggy back.)

But their delight was short-lived as some very unfriendly looking villagers emerged. They threw the Cycloctopus a huge carcass, which it ate in a single bite before it slithered away.

"It must be some kind of 'guard squid'," said Gene.

"We are the um-Fruitbat People of Smell Dorado. You um-come to meet the chief," said one of the villagers. "You no um-run away!"

And with that, Gerald, Gene and Fleabag were led into the village.

And everything was made of gold – the houses, the shops, the benches, even the paving stones! But this was no ordinary gold... This gold had a strange putrid colour and gave off a foul odour.

"Green gold?!" said Gene. "I've never seen anything like this before."

"And that *smell*," said Gerald, wincing. "No wonder you don't find it on jewellery."

After a short walk they arrived at the chief's house – and the chief did not look happy!

"I am Chief Fruitum," he said. "We um-guard the bog while the um-monkeys guard the jungle. And no one who um-walks on our um-land goes unpunished..."

"But we can explain," said Gene. "We have the—"

"Silence!" said Fruitum. "For your um-impertinence you must suffer the **Fate of a Thousand Creepy Crawlies**! Now, prepare the pit!"

The villagers led Gerald, Gene and Fleabag Monkeyface to the town square, where they placed them neck deep in a pit of the vilest, grossest creepy crawlies imaginable...

"Well, Hotel Dorado doesn't seem so bad now," said Gerald as a slug the size of a puppy crawled over his head.

"Yes, and that swimming pool actually seems like it would be quite fun," said Gene as an earwig with pincers the size of nail scissors tweaked his nose.

"Hey, it's not so ug-bad," said Fleabag as a snail the size of a rucksack crawled up his neck.

If you're finding this all a bit too disgusting, here is a page from the Smugleys' pressed flower album to make you feel better...

Cupcake
Orchid

Fairy Wing
Daisy

Kitten
Rose

19 "I hope you've got a plan," said Gerald.

"I did," said Gene. "But it involved Gross-Out Power..."

All that could be seen of Fleabag was the tuft of hair on the very top of his head.

"And we were so close to saving the world," said Gerald, taking a final glance at the rucksack containing the **Golden Toilet**.

"We need a miracle," said Gene.

Suddenly, there was a screech of brakes and a friendly face appeared at the rim of the pit.

"Montana!" cried Gerald.

"Good thing I know all the short cuts in this place. Now hurry! We don't have much time!" said the intrepid explorer. "Grab hold of my whip!" And one by one Montana hauled them from the pit.

They ran to Montana's jeep as dozens of angry natives emerged from their huts. Montana slammed his foot down on the accelerator and the car lurched away with the locals in pursuit.

Iggy bravely crawled down Fleabag's arm and threw himself at the locals ...

... as Montana swerved past market stalls ...

ZOOM!

... through houses ...

... and past axe-wielding natives ...

SMASH!

... until they finally burst through the village gates.

"Now on to the Temple of Baboon," said Montana.

"But how did you escape from the baron's cage?" asked Gene.

"For weeks I have been cutting away at the bars with a saw," Montana explained.

"A saw! Why did it take so ug-long?" asked Fleabag.

"It was no ordinary saw," said Montana, holding up a tiny implement. "It's a traditional rice-saw that I unearthed while excavating the villages of the Mouldcutter People of Saraquak. They use it to slice and dice grains of rice."

"So the baron knows the Toilet is missing?" said Gene.

"Oh yes," said Montana. "And by my calculations he may well get to the Temple before us. He knows that's where we'll head. Now hold on tight: we're going off-road!"

Meanwhile, Baron Von Dirthoffen and Melvin were almost at the Temple.

"Ve cannot afford any slip-ups," said the baron, looking at the sky. "It is almost time for the eclipse. We must get the Toilet back now! Hit ze helicopter button, Melvin! I have a plan – but first we need to enter ze temple."

As they approached the Temple of Baboon, an army of monkeys, led by the Baboon King, who was looking resplendent in his feathered headdress and robes, began shooting arrows at the Grossempole.

"We can't take too much of this," said Melvin.

"Operate ze grabbing hand and grab the king!" ordered the baron. "Once we have him, their morale vill plummet and they vill all just become frightened little chimpies!"

Melvin directed the Grossempole's huge mechanical hand over the king.

"NOW!!!!" Von Dirthoffen bellowed.

The metal hand slammed into a fist – they had captured the king! And as the baron had predicted, the remaining monkey soldiers were soon beating a hasty retreat.

"The Temple is secure! Now all we have to do is vait for those fools to deliver the **Golden Toilet** straight to daddy!" Von Dirthoffen cackled. "And, look, ve have just about enough time for *ein* sausage snack!"

21 After bumping along endless pot-holed dirt tracks, Montana, Gerald, Gene and Fleabag were nearing the end of their journey.

Up ahead was the **Temple of Baboon**!

"Looks like we beat Von Dirthoffen!" said Gerald. "There's no sign of the Grossempole."

"This place is quiet ... too quiet," said Montana nervously. "There should be guards here."

"I ug-smell trouble," said Fleabag, his nostrils flaring.

"We need to get to the main hall – the king should be there. We don't have long to get the Toilet back," said Montana, looking up at the sky.

They hurried through the Temple to the main hall.

And there, waiting for them on the Baboon King's throne, was the gruesome grossaeologist!

"Vell, look who we have here!" he gloated. "I knew you vould deliver the Toilet straight back to me!"

"Never!" cried Montana. "We are here to return it to the king. What are you doing on his throne?"

Before the baron could answer, there was a loud crash and the Grossempole smashed through a wall of the Temple.

"Grab ze toilet!" the baron shouted.

Melvin once again operated the Grossempole's grabbing hand, and this time the target was Gene's rucksack and its precious contents.

"Don't let him get the Toilet!" cried Montana.

But the Grossempole was too quick, and before Fleabag could muster up so much as a turbo fart, they had all been captured.

107

"Like taking candy from *ein* baby," said the baron, plucking the rucksack from Gene's back. "Now drop zem in the caves beneath the Temple, Melvin, where they can't interfere *mit mein* plan."

"Your plan?" asked Montana.

"I might as vell tell you," said the baron. "Under *mein* command, the Zombie Monkeys will ransack every museum in the vorld, *und* then I will fill them *mit mein* own gross-out artefacts. I vill be so much more than *ein* Travelling Showman!"

"You'll never get away with it!" said Gene.

"I already have," said the baron, lifting up a metal grate. A terrible smell wafted into the room.

GROAN!

"What is that stench?" Gerald grimaced.

"And what is that noise?" asked Fleabag as hideous groaning noises filled the room.

"It's the Dungataur," Montana moaned.

AND I AM SURE ZE DUNGATAUR WOULD LIKE SOME LUNCH. IT IS PRETTY HUNGRY WORK BEING HALF-HUMAN *UND* HALF-DUNG BEETLE!!!! RELEASE THEM INTO THE PIT, MELVIN.

As instructed, Melvin released the grabbing hand, and the foursome tumbled into a great abyss.

"*Und* now let us go to the top of *das* Temple," said the baron. "I want to be on high to command *mein* army of Zombie Monkeys!!!"

The baron and Melvin took the precious Toilet to the Temple's summit, while deep underground, Montana and the boys had landed on a huge dung heap. They were in the creepiest hole any of them had ever seen.

 **22** "We need to get out of here – and fast!" urged Montana. "The Dungataur is the most dangerous creature in the whole kingdom and these caverns are an unsolvable maze."

Just then there was a cave-shuddering growl.

GRRRRR!

"What do we do?" shrieked Gene.

"Quick," said Montana. "Legend tells of a map carved on the wall of the innermost chamber. We have to find it!"

Suddenly, the noise behind them got louder.

"Oh no," groaned Montana. "The Dungataur has released its deadliest weapon..."

Gerald, Gene and Fleabag looked round.

A huge dung ball was thundering down the tunnel behind them! Not only that, but in front of them, the path was about to come to an abrupt end...

"The Chasm of Doom!" gasped Montana. "No one has ever crossed it."

"Ug-hold on to me!" said Fleabag, shooting out a length of nose hair. It caught around a stalactite.

Grabbing hold of the hair, the four of them swung out over the abyss. They landed in a heap on the other side. Behind them, the huge dung ball crashed down into the darkness.

"That was close," said Gerald. "Look, the Dungataur is stuck on the other side. We're safe!"

"And we're in the innermost chamber!" Montana smiled, dusting himself down.

"And look, the map!" said Gene, pointing at the wall behind them.

Can you help Montana, Gerald, Gene and Fleabag find their way out? Beware: there are lots of booby traps!

VAMPIRE BATS

PIRANHA
LAKE

CROCODILE
LAIR

EXIT

Congratulations! You have safely made it
through the cave!

The four adventurers emerged blinking into the daylight. They had escaped the **Great Maze of the Dungataur**, but in the sky the moon was about to cover the sun.

"We're too late," said Montana. "The baron has won!"

"We're not beaten yet," said a voice behind them. "And *he* can change everything." It was the caged Baboon King and he was pointing at Fleabag.

23 "**Z**is trip to Smell Dorado really hasn't been so bad." Von Dirthoffen cackled as he and Melvin reached the very top of the Temple. "I have *mein* toilet back, the Zombie Monkeys will soon appear and be at my command, and best of all I have got rid of that pesky Montana Smith *und* those kids once *und* for all!"

"And now ze solar eclipse is just minutes away!" the baron added, putting the Toilet on the ground. "The time has come!"

"The world's greatest grossaeologist will soon be a household name." Melvin beamed. "And the tills in every great museum in the world will ring out for us for ever!!!"

"Now," said the baron, stroking his chin. "I think we have just about enough time for *ein* bratwurst nibble..."

24

"**W**hat do you mean that Fleabag can change everything?" Gene asked the Baboon King.

"In Ancient Baboonian legend, there is a story of a great warrior monkey," explained the king. "He is called **Chimpzilla** and it was he who defeated the Zombie Monkeys and banished them underground."

"Of course!" cried Gene, remembering the note in Gerald's guidebook. "All we need is the **Elixir of Yuck** and Fleabag will become Chimpzilla."

"Alas, the elixir was lost many years ago," the Baboon King sighed. "But if Fleabag puts on the helmet that I wear under my headdress..."

Fleabag put on the helmet ... and the resemblance to Chimpzilla was astonishing!

"Now we need an army," said Gene.

"An army needs a leader and with me locked in this cage things looked hopeless – but now the Great Chimpzilla is back..." said the Baboon King, before letting off a jungle-shuddering screech.

Dozens of monkeys and Fruitbat People started to emerge from the trees. They all bowed to Fleabag. Their great leader had returned to save them!

THE GREAT CHIMPZILLA HAS RETURNED. WE WILL OBEY YOU, OH MASTER!

"This is ug-great!" said Fleabag. "Now for an ug-inspiring speech: IT IS A GREAT UG-HONOUR TO ADDRESS YOU TODAY AS YOUR UG-LEADER. THERE IS AN UG-EPIC BATTLE AHEAD AND I UG-THINK OF THE WORDS OF MY SCHOOL TEACHER MR UG-TROUTMAN..."

"There's no time for this," said Montana. "We need to defeat the baron!"

Fleabag led his army to the top of the Temple...
But it was too late.

The skies had darkened, the solar eclipse had
begun – and the baron had said the spell... The
Zombie Monkeys were under his command!

"Look who it is!" he boomed, spying Montana,
Gerald, Gene and Fleabag. "So you survived the
Dungataur! *Und* the ape-boy has got *ein* new hat!
Well, you are too late! Zombie Monkeys – ATTACK!!!"

Fleabag unleashed an earth-shattering turbo fart –
but even his **Gross-Out Powers** were no match for
the zombies. The army was soon forced back.

"It's no ug-good," yelped Fleabag. "They are just
too ug-strong!"

"Let's get out of here!" added Gerald.

"See how zey flee!" scoffed the baron. "Now, *mein*
monkeys, destroy ze Temple. Then we can get out
of here!"

25

Fleabag and the others scampered back to the king. The Chimpzilla plan had failed!

They were all feeling very dejected until the king suddenly exclaimed, "Wait!" and pointed at the small glass bottle hanging around Montana's neck. "Where did you get that?"

"It was given to me by a native the last time I was here," said Montana. "I didn't realize it was valuable."

"*Valuable*?! It's priceless. It's the **Elixir of Yuck**!" said the Baboon King. "That potion had been passed down through my family for centuries until I lost it in the jungle. Now we can invoke the ancient spirit of the warrior monkey **Chimpzilla**!"

"The Elixir of Ug-Yuck – make mine a double!" said Fleabag enthusiastically.

"Very well," said the king, opening the bottle and pouring the precious liquid on to an ornate spoon. "Now, open wide. Here comes the **Baboon Spoon**."

As soon as Fleabag had gulped down the liquid, he felt power surge through his entire body...

His arms bulged...

His legs grew...

And his whole body swelled up.

With his new-found super-strength he was ready to take on the Zombie Monkeys and their evil commander.

"Back to ug-battle, my monkeys-in-arms!" he cried.

Fleabag now swatted the zombies away with ease. The baron and his nephew retreated into the Grossempole. "I have activated the Grossempole force field, Uncle," said Melvin. "Anything that touches us will receive a massive electric shock!"

But the supercharged Fleabag had no fear of force fields or electric shocks, and with an **enormous bionic belch**, he toppled the dastardly vehicle!

See how the Zombie Monkeys flee! he cried.

And, sure enough, most of the zombies were already heading back down the Toilet.

They were terrified of their arch enemy Chimpzilla!

"I'm not finished yet!" said the deranged grossaeologist. "Come back, zombies! I command you!"

At the command of their master, some of the zombies re-emerged from the Toilet. But Fleabag lifted the Grossempole clear off the ground and turbo-farted it to the entrance of the Dungataur's cave.

"This is your last ug-chance, Baron," he said. "Order the Zombie Monkeys to leave or you will be ug-Dungataur food!"

"Very vell," said Baron Von Dirthoffen. "You win again, Montana. **ZOMBIE MONKEYS, RETURN TO THE UNDERGROUND KINGDOM!!!**"

The remaining zombies immediately started jumping into the **Golden Toilet**, and one by one they vanished back from whence they came.

Fleabag had saved the day!

26 Having captured Melvin and Baron Von Dirthoffen, Montana, Gerald, Gene and Fleabag were ready to go home.

"How can we ever thank you?" said the Baboon King.

"Actually, you could help us back to the hotel," said Gerald. "My parents will be wondering where we are."

"First we must seal the gates so no one can ever steal the **Golden Toilet** again," said Montana.

"But how?" asked Gerald.

"I think I have an idea..." said Gene.

"That should do it," said Fleabag, once the Grossempole was in position by the gates.

"Now," Gene explained to the Baboon King, "you just need to push the Grossempole up against the gates once we're gone and Smell Dorado will be safe for ever!"

"We will make sure the zombies are never unleashed again," said the king as he waved them off.

But as the foursome headed back towards the river, they heard a plaintive cry.

"Help!" said a tiny voice.

"We've been calling out for hours," said another voice.

"What now?" sighed Montana.

"Oh, it's just the Smugleys and our rafting guide." Gene chuckled as he spotted the twins and Ernesto stuck in a huge plant.

"That's a giant Venus flytrap," said Montana. "It must have escaped from the **Valley of Putrid Plants**."

131

They soon cut the Smugleys and Ernesto free. Fortunately, they were too traumatized by their run-in with a man-eating plant to ask many questions.

Everyone clambered into the raft, and in no time they were back at the hotel. It was time to say goodbye to Montana.

"Guys, I could never have done this without you," the explorer said. "The first stop for me is the police station with these two. Their museum days are over."

"Then ug-what, Mr Smith?" asked Fleabag. "Why not ug-join us at the hotel? It's Hawaiian Pizza and ug-Cabaret Night. All the pineapple and pizza you can eat. And hula skirts too!"

"I'd love to, but an explorer never stands still – and I've been in a cage too long. There is a legend that the Ruined Palace of Columzuela is home to a lost emerald potty... I'll give you a shout if I need a hand!"

And with that he was gone...

"So how was your rafting trip?" Gerald's dad asked as they sat down to dinner that night.

"It's a long story." Gerald laughed.

"Well, I for one am glad to be going home tomorrow," said Gerald's mum. "I think we're all excursioned-out. Sorry if you boys have found things a bit boring."

"Boring?" said Gene. "It's actually been surprisingly interesting..."

27 The next evening they were finally back.

"Home sweet ug-home," said Fleabag as they got to the door of the Den.

"Well, that's a holiday we won't forget in a hurry," said Gerald. "Shame we didn't get to buy any souvenirs."

"Come on, Fleabag," said Gene. "Open the door. I'm dying to see the Den again."

But the door to the Gross-Out Den wouldn't open.

In the end, they all had to climb through the window – and once inside, they soon discovered what had been blocking the door.

"The place is full of boxes," said Gene.

"It's all the ug-stuff I ordered from the museum," said Fleabag. "Montana must have forwarded it on: Seventeen 'I've been to Baron Von Dirthoffen's Travelling Museum' T-Shirts, fourteen ug-replica Phoenician nose-pickers, twelve Inca potty deity statuettes and thirty-five Smell Dorado snow shakers!"

"Montana is splitting the baron's collection between the great museums of the world," said Gene, reading the attached letter. "At least now more museums will have gross-out exhibits!"

"And we have plenty of souvenirs!" Gerald laughed. "Look – he even returned our film gear!"

To find out what the trio decide to film, you'll need to read the next "Disgusting Adventure of Fleabag Monkeyface" – which makes this one look like a luxury spa in a five-star hotel! **Don't say we didn't warn you!!!**

If you can't wait until the next Fleabag Monkeyface book, here's a free comic to keep you going. (It makes perfect on-the-toilet reading!)

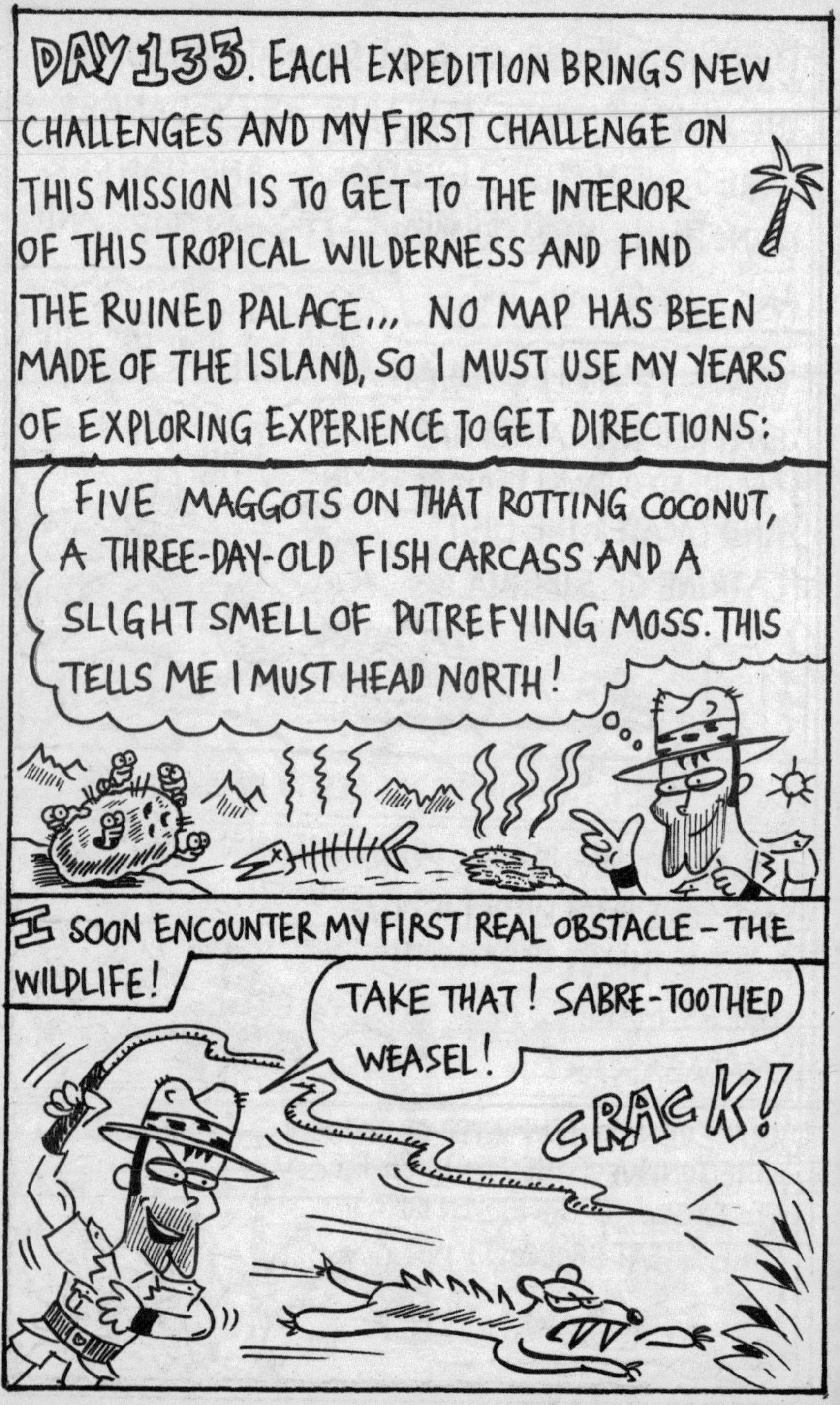
DAY 133. EACH EXPEDITION BRINGS NEW CHALLENGES AND MY FIRST CHALLENGE ON THIS MISSION IS TO GET TO THE INTERIOR OF THIS TROPICAL WILDERNESS AND FIND THE RUINED PALACE... NO MAP HAS BEEN MADE OF THE ISLAND, SO I MUST USE MY YEARS OF EXPLORING EXPERIENCE TO GET DIRECTIONS:
FIVE MAGGOTS ON THAT ROTTING COCONUT, A THREE-DAY-OLD FISH CARCASS AND A SLIGHT SMELL OF PUTREFYING MOSS. THIS TELLS ME I MUST HEAD NORTH!
I SOON ENCOUNTER MY FIRST REAL OBSTACLE – THE WILDLIFE!
TAKE THAT! SABRE-TOOTHED WEASEL!
CRACK!